To Kit

with love

from

Rob
x

Joe & Dusty

Save the World

For Ciarain
who was kind.

For Dusty
who is laughter.

And for Hormoz
who is love.

First published 2021 by Joe and Dusty Books. Text © 2021 Robert Martin. Illustrations © 2021 Margit van der Zwan.

The right of Robert Martin to be identified as the author, and Margit van der Zwan to be identified as the illustrator, of this work has been asserted by them in accordance with the Copyright, Designs and Patents Act 1988.

Design by Anne Louise Kershaw, Instigate Arts CIC www. instigatearts.org

Printed by Vegan Print, meaning it is fully vegan and has been made in a way that is socially and environmentally responsible. www.veganprint.co.uk

Welcome to the world of Joe & Dusty

It's a world in which the most important things in life are kindness, laughter and, above all, love.

For their first adventure, Joe and Dusty Save the World, it's these very things that get them through a really tricky situation, one which sees the whole planet depending on them.

In my life, kindness, laughter and love are the things that have helped get me and those I care about through our own tricky situations.

Joe is a boy who is differently abled. I have known lots of people with different abilities, including one of my sisters, so

I know that everyone is unique in their own way. That's why my story isn't just about Joe's abilities, it's about HIM!

And it's about Dusty, because she's my dog in real life and she fills me with the laughter, kindness and love that helped to inspire this story.

Look out for more Joe and Dusty adventures and thank you for being a kind person and reading my book.

Robert Martin

Meet Joe & Dusty

This is Joe!

He's a differently abled boy who loves to have adventures with Dusty, his best friend.

This is Dusty!

She's an English Bull Terrier and Joe's best pal, but she also looks after him when he needs it.

Dusty helps Joe with some of his special needs. When Joe feels anxious or worried, Dusty helps him. When Joe feels nervous, unsure or upset, Dusty reassures him.

Most of the time they just enjoy being together and having fun, but she's always there to make him feel OK.

And some of our friends

Heroes come in all shapes and sizes. Joe and Dusty are a great example of this. We need different people to make the world better in lots of different ways. don't know what the future holds but I know everyone has potential. And wherever our adventures take us we'll need different people to help save the day.

When I was young I loved reading books and telling stories. I hope this book helps more young people fall in love with reading. And that it helps everyone see the world needs all kinds of heroes, like Joe and Dusty and me and you!

Sarah Gordy MBE

Welcome to the wonderful world of Joe and Dusty, superheroes with a difference!

What a beautiful idea this is: to put a child with learning differences, and his dog companion, at the centre of the action, literally saving the world with the underrated superpowers of love, friendship, music, dancing....and even farts.

All these things feature in Joe and Dusty Save the World, as do silly aliens who have to learn how to FEEL. Imagine! It is a lovely book, with funny illustrations and an IMPORTANT MESSAGE. Hooray for underrated superpowers and the healing magic of love. I hope you enjoy it as much as I did.

Julie Hesmondhalgh

Chapter 1

The story I'm about to tell
Is one full of surprise.
A really strange adventure that will
Make you wide of eyes.

You'll take deep breaths, you'll laugh out loud,
Or even jump with fright,
But do not fret, because our tale
Is going to delight.

It's all about a boy named Joe
And Dusty, his best friend.
The love between this boy and dog
Would never, ever end.

Dusty was a Terrier,
Her type, an English Bull,
And since she'd been a puppy she had
Made Joe's heart feel full.

For they were close as close can be,
Their friendship knew no bounds.
Joe knew that he was lucky to have
Met the best of hounds.

You see, she wasn't just a pet,
She often helped with things,
When Joe was anxious, sad or cross,
Confused or wandering.

Dusty had been trained to act
As Joe's four-legged helper,
To calm his nerves, to guide the way,
And never be a yelper.

She calmly understood just when
Joe needed extra care –
She'd look at him and start to wag
Her tail in the air.

She'd use her skills when she could sense
In Joe some apprehension.
She'd comfort him, and make him safe,
And focus his attention,

Right back to where he felt OK,
Forgetting all his fear.
Dusty had the power to make
His worries disappear.

Sometimes to play a game was just
The thing to make it right,
At other times to snuggle as they
Fell asleep at night.

For Joe had needs that meant he often
Felt a little distant
From other kids he knew at school,
Although they weren't resistant

To being friends, including Joe
In all their games and races.
But Joe preferred his peace and quiet
And sought out gentle places.

He didn't really like the kinds of
Violent games they played –
Explosions, noise and fighting made him
Feel quite dismayed.

7

Soldiers, spacemen, running, chasing,
Monsters, zombies, ghouls,
Using guns and bombs and other
Kinds of nasty tools.

On screens, his friends would gather points
To give them superpowers,
Then use them just to blow things up
For hours and hours and hours.

Joe enjoyed much calmer things
Like tending to his herbs,
Like planting in his garden,
Like listening to the birds.

He loved it in the summer when
The bees came, all a-buzzy.
When butterflies flew next to him,
It made him warm and fuzzy.

And sometimes in the dark Joe loved
To look up at the sky,
Hoping that he'd see a shooting star
Go flying by.

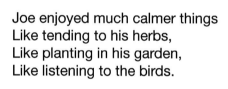

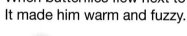

For when Joe's thoughts got cloudy or
Banged around like thunder,
Looking at the moon and stars
Filled him full of wonder.

Looking at the universe
Oh so high above
Made Joe calm, remembering
All the things he loved.

He loved his mum, he loved his dad,
He loved his sisters too.
He loved to play his favourite songs
Whilst sitting on the loo.

He loved to play a game of chase
With Dusty in the park,
To watch and laugh when squirrels made her
Run away and bark.

Joe and Dusty fitted like
A hand inside a glove.
It isn't hard to understand
Joe's superpower was LOVE.

Yet Joe's heart had a single wish
He wanted to come true.
He wished that Dusty had the power
To speak, although he knew

That dogs can't talk like people can.
But if he had a choice,
He'd really love to hear the sound of
Dusty's doggy voice.

So now you know this story is
About a boy called Joe,
And Dusty too… but WAIT, there's something else
You need to know.

Before our story proper starts,
A secret must be told,
Something that's important to
The way things will unfold.

A thing so big it makes all else seem
Like a bit, "whatever".
Something that will change the way
You think and feel, forever.

So sit right down, take deep breaths
And please try not to squeal.
The thing you have to know is
ALIENS ARE REAL!

Yes, that's right, they do exist,
So now you know the truth,
And Joe and Dusty's story will
Provide you with the proof.

Perhaps you've heard of UFOs,
Seen films where vicious creatures
Invade the earth and frighten people
With their ugly features.

Or played a game where blowing up
The aliens is cool,
Pretending you're a soldier,
Just like Joe's friends at school.

But games and films and TV shows
And comic books don't tell
The truth about the aliens –
Perhaps that's just as well.

Out in space there are so many
Types of alien -
Some are just like reptiles,
Some, mammalian.

Some are blobs of gooey stuff,
Others look like flies,
But the ones that visit us
You might well recognise.

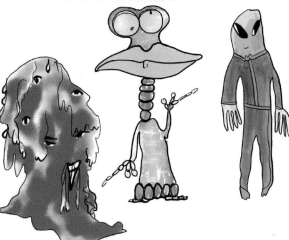

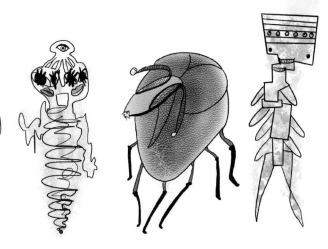

And that's because you've seen them when
You're walking home at night,
They're hiding in the bushes,
Barely out of sight.

Tingling all your senses till you
Turn your head around,
You shout 'Hello' but they stand still
And never make a sound.

You see strange lights up in the sky,
'It's just a plane,' you say,
But then the lights start following,
As you go on your way.

You walk a little quicker and get home,
All full of dread,
But they're looking through your window
As you lie asleep in bed.

They fly here in their spaceships,
Hiding in the clouds,
Waiting till it's quiet and
Avoiding any crowds.

You see, for many years they have been
Visiting the Earth,
Watching what we're up to,
Seeing if it's worth

Risking what they value most –
People not believing
That aliens are real.
So they just keep retrieving

Loads of information
Which is all designed to trace,
The very odd behaviour
Of the human race.

Waiting till the time is right to use their
Spaceship's phone
To give the planet Earth a call and say
'You're not alone.'

But lately things have caused our visitors
From space to worry,
To get back in their UFOs and
Leave us in a hurry.

The aliens have noticed that there's something
That has changed,
Something that they do not not like,
Something very strange.

This leads us to our story,
Which now can be unfurled,
Of how a boy named Joe, and his dog Dusty,
Saved the world.

Chapter 2

It all began one summer's day,
A day like all the rest.
Nothing was unusual
As Joe got home and pressed

His finger on the front door bell,
Ringing out its chime,
So Dusty would get ready
For Joe and Dusty time!

For every day when Joe got home,
Dusty ran to meet him.
He'd fall down upon the floor so
She could lick and greet him.

They'd roll around and tumble,
Then they'd hurtle down the hall,
Out into the garden, where
Into the grass they'd fall.

This is what would happen when Joe
Came from school each day.
With lots of hugs and cuddles,
Joe and Dusty loved to play.

Sometimes it was hide-and-seek,
Or just a game of chase,
Sometimes Joe just liked to find
A still and quiet place

Where they could smell the flowers,
Side by side they'd lie,
Listening to the birds or watching
Clouds above roll by.

Joe and Dusty's daily playtime
Filled their hearts with joy,
For no bond was as special as
Between this dog and boy.

And from the kitchen window,
Joe's mum and dad could see
That special bond, and it would always
Fill their hearts with glee.

Joe's parents sometimes joined them,
And his sisters, one two three,
Spending time together before
Sitting down for tea.

Six o'clock was dinner,
Time to talk about their day,
What they'd learned at school or maybe
Games they'd liked to play.

Joe's three sisters started and
First of all was Lily,
She really loved to dance ballet
In dresses pink and frilly.

She made it look so easy as she
Danced with grace and style,
But it took hard work and focus and
She practised all the while.

Sometimes Joe would practise too
Just for fun with Lily,
But they'd always end up laughing,
And make the dances silly.

Next was Skye who couldn't wait to
Tell them her report,
Of all of her successes in her
Favourite pastime – sport!

She always loved to win but knew
The way to get your dream,
Was helping everybody work
Together as a team.

18

Skye saw that in teamwork every
Problem could be solved.
She showed Joe that things are best
When everyone's involved.

As for little Harper, far too
Young to go to school,
She made everybody laugh
By acting like a fool!

When Joe was feeling sad, well, she could
Make him laugh for hours.
And so, you see, Joe's sisters all had
Their own superpowers!

After dinner, they would play until
Their sleepy eyes,
Told them that the time had come
To go to beddy-byes.

Every evening Joe would need to
Follow his routine,
First it was pyjamas,
Next his teeth to clean!

Then it would be time to make
A visit to the loo –
He couldn't sleep until he'd had
A bedtime wee or poo.

Finally, a thorough wash,
Then into bed he'd snuggle.
You see, without routine Joe often
Found things quite a struggle.

When things were new or different,
Joe could feel off track,
But Dusty knew the way to help him
Find his way right back.

Three more things Joe needed
As to sleep he fell,
His glasses and his mobile phone
And lastly, can you tell?

20

Number three was someone upon
Whom he could depend,
To stay with him all through the night –
Dusty, his best friend.

She'd jump right up upon the bed
So they could have a cuddle,
Then Joe would lift the duvet and
Down by his feet she'd snuggle.

Mum and Dad would hug him hard and
Kiss him nighty-night,
Then Joe would get his phone out before
Turning off the light.

He'd put the headphones on and listen
To his favourite songs,
Looking at the photos he'd been taking
All day long.

Selfies with his family,
Friends and Dusty too.
Helping him remember all the
Things he liked to do.

And just before he nodded off,
While he was still able,
He'd remove his glasses, put them
On the bedside table.

He'd have a stretch, switch off his phone,
Then he'd sleep till dawn.
The last thing that he heard each night was
Dusty's sleepy yawn.

And so it was this very night,
A night when nothing strange
Could ever have suggested that
Everything would change.

For when they would awaken, Dusty,
And her best friend Joe,
Would not be in their bedroom,
But on board a UFO…

Chapter 3

Dusty's powerful nose was first
To notice something wrong.
Normally she woke up smelling
Joe's feet – what a pong!

Before her eyes had opened,
Her cold wet nose was twitching.
There was something new to smell,
Something quite bewitching.

From the covers, Dusty yawned and
Poked her head from under,
But straight away her ears pricked up,
Her heart – it beat like thunder.

This was not the bedroom where
They'd gone to sleep last night.
This was just an empty space
Where everything was white.

So Dusty, being oh so brave,
Jumped from the bed, all cosy,
To follow where the smell came from
'Cos Dusty, she was nosy.

With one glance back at Joe she thought,
Without a hesitation,
That she had to keep him safe
Through dog investigation!

Once she set her mind to something,
Nothing else could goad her,
And off she boldly went to find
The source of this new odour.

Not long after, something made Joe
Wake from his repose.
Usually it would be Dusty
Licking at his toes.

Joe sat up and rubbed his eyes then
Reached out from the bed –
His glasses would be either on
The table or his head.

He waved his arm around to try
And find the bedside table,
But no matter how he searched
He simply wasn't able.

How had it just disappeared?
Vanished in thin air?
Joe sat upright wondering
What else wasn't there!

Without his glasses, all that he could see
Was brilliant white.
Clearly something very strange had
Happened overnight.

Where were all his things? His room?
And more importantly,
The fundamental question was,
Where on Earth was he?

Normally Joe's day began with
Slobbering and kissing,
And that was when he realised
That Dusty too was missing.

'Dusty! Dusty!' he called out,
Then through the silence, Hark!
Sounding not too far away,
Joe heard Dusty bark.

Joe jumped out of bed to where there
Should have been a mat.
That's the place where usually his
Slippers would have sat.

The cold floor made him shiver,
Because his feet were bare,
And though he hated being cold,
Today he didn't care.

Because, though you might think these things
Could easily have made
Joe feel scared and anxious,
He was not afraid.

And that's because his overriding
Need to find his dog,
Helped to calm and guide him,
Like a lighthouse in the fog.

Hands outstretched to help him find
His way through blurry eyes,
Joe had no idea just how
Big of a surprise

Waited for him as he slowly
Walked along the walls,
Feeling his way through a door,
Down corridors and halls.

Everywhere was clean and smooth
And everything was bright.
It made it hard to find the way,
Like when it's dark at night.

27

But then, at last, Joe came into
A room where he could hear
Dusty gently growling at
Someone who was near.

Squinting, Joe saw what he thought were
Children playing Statue,
A game where you stand oh so still
'Till someone's running at you.

'Hello? Who's there? And have you seen
My glasses 'cos they've gone?
And now I don't know where I am
And can't see anyone!'

Dusty ran to Joe, then turned around
With her best scowl.
That's when Joe thought, 'Aaah, they must be
Frightened of her growl!'

And then a voice that sounded like
A robot, monotone,
Said, 'Yes we have your glasses,
But we thought you were alone.

'You really should not be awake,
That's not the way things go.
And a dog was hiding in your bed.
How were we to know?

'She ran in and growled at us
And backed us in a corner.
We've never met a dog before
So will you kindly warn her,

'To please refrain from growling at us.
Look at all that slime!
We can tell she's thinking that we're
Her next dinner-time!'

'Oh don't worry,' Joe said.
'Dusty's growls are just pretend.
She wants to know if it's OK
For you to be my friend.'

29

Joe looked down at Dusty
And she looked up at Joe.
He smiled and said, 'It's all OK.'
That's all she had to know.

So Dusty tried to smile at them,
But it was really hard.
She'd never seen an alien and still
Was on her guard.

(Plus they smelt so tasty and her
Nose was not for fooling,
So her attempts to smile were
Accompanied by drooling!)

Still Joe felt the start of feelings
Warning him of dangers
That he often felt when he was
In a place with strangers.

Now, when it came to feelings, well,
Joe had them all a-plenty.
Sometimes if he was anxious he would breathe
And count to twenty

As a way to calm himself
When things felt uncontrolled,
And as he counted he remembered
What he had been told.

His parents always said to him,
'Joe if you should ever
Find that you are somewhere strange
With Dusty, you should never

'Feel lost or frightened,
As she will guide you home.'
And so Joe knew that with his dog,
He'd never be alone.

Joe was someone filled with kindness,
Love and true affection,
And he knew that Dusty was right there
For his protection.

He thought about his garden, how the
Flowers smelled so calming.
It always helped relax him
When things seemed so alarming.

He felt quite safe, and still was unaware
Of his abduction.
So just one thing was missing –
A proper introduction!

He smiled and shouted, 'Hi, I'm Joe!
And Dusty, she won't eat you.
Won't you come on over so that
I can hug and meet you?'

From the group, the one who'd spoken
Walked towards the twosome,
Even though it thought that Dusty's smile
Was pretty gruesome!

Joe could see more clearly what was
Just a child, he thought.
It seemed a little different,
Its legs seemed rather short,

Its head seemed big, its eyes were too,
He couldn't see a nose,
And there was another thing –
What was it with their clothes?

But Joe had friends with differences
Far too wide to name,
So he just treated everyone
Like we are all the same.

Some were deaf, some used wheelchairs
To get around,
Some had other needs as well,
But Joe had always found

It hard to understand
When people couldn't hide,
Looking at you strangely,
When you're just you inside.

And even though he knew it wasn't
Right to hold a grudge,
Joe liked animals the best -
Animals don't judge.

Long and slender hands returned
Joe's glasses to his eyes.
And alien and boy just stood there,
Speechless with surprise.

The alien was shocked because
Joe still wasn't screaming.
Joe was shocked because he really thought
He must be dreaming.

He knew that they were aliens,
He'd seen them in the games
That Skye, his sister, sometimes played,
But this was not the same.

Here they were in real life,
And Joe began to feel
That this was not a dream at all,
This was all too real.

Dusty, who was just as clever
As a dog could be,
Sensed that Joe was getting scared and
Wondered, how could she

Make him feel safe and help to
Ease his mind so puzzled?
She wagged her tail, licked his hand,
Which then she gently nuzzled.

With friendly face, she quietly tried to
Capture his attention.
She knew that if he looked into her eyes,
That all his tension,

All his worries and concerns and
All his new-found fear,
Would fade away as she helped
It all to disappear.

Joe looked down at Dusty and it
Made him feel calmer.
She turned towards the alien, she knew
It wouldn't harm her.

And because she wagged her tail at it,
And seemed so unafraid,
Joe felt, maybe, this was just a
New friend to be made.

So alien and boy stood staring
Silently, apart,
And that's when cheeky Dusty did
A great big massive fart.

It made a noise like when the air
Flies from a balloon,
And suddenly, its eggy smell
Entirely filled the room.

Never had the aliens smelt something
So horrific.
But Joe thought Dusty's trumps were always
Funny and terrific.

Because they made him laugh so much,
And he let out a giggle,
Dusty thought it was a game,
Her tail began to wiggle.

The aliens were pulling faces,
Feeling nauseous,
Which just made Joe laugh more.
How hilarious!

'What is that smell? Please make it stop.'
The alien's voice pleaded.
But a little laughter had been
Just the thing Joe needed.

'It's just a fart,' Joe shouted,
'It came from Dusty's bum.
Sometimes they sound like little squeaks
And sometimes like a drum!'

The alien said, 'Catch the fart and
We can test it later,
Examine it so we can add our findings
To our data.'

'You can't catch a fart,' Joe laughed,
'Now can you please explain,
Where on Earth I am right now,
And do you have name?'

But Joe and Dusty weren't on Earth,
Though they still didn't know it.
They were flying out in space,
And it was time to show it.

34

Chapter 4

Now, all the little aliens,
They just weren't used to this.
It was their final mission and
Things had gone amiss.

For many years they'd visited
The Earth from outer space,
Studying and finding out
About the human race.

Sometimes they would just observe,
Getting confirmation
Of all their years of data
And heaps of information.

Occasionally, they would have to
Beam a person up,
But they had never beamed on board
A person with a pup.

Fast asleep, supposedly,
The people would remain,
Waking up next day like everything
Was just the same.

Sometimes, if a person beamed on board
Woke with a fright,
The aliens had power to make
Everything all right.

Amazingly, they had a special
Way to make it seem
Like it hadn't really happened,
Like it was all a dream.

Lots of people had been beamed aboard,
But never knew,
And just imagine, maybe even
One of them was YOU!

Surprised that Joe was still so calm
And hadn't screamed with fear,
The alien came closer
Until it was quite near.

By now, it thought, most humans would be
Terrified at best,
But it sensed that Joe was somewhat
Different from the rest.

'I asked you a question.
Can you answer it?' said Joe.
'Where am I and who are you?
I'd really like to know.'

The alien, all oval-faced with
Great big massive eyes,
Said in its robotic voice,
'This may be a surprise.

'There's no need to be afraid,
We do not mean you harm.
But I must tell you something which
Could cause you some alarm.

'You are not on Earth at all.
We've travelled from a place
A million miles away from here,
The other side of space.

'It is our job to gather
Information that is new.
Last night we brought you here because
We chose to study you.

'You are on board our spaceship
As we circle round the moon.
But now it's gone all wrong, so we must
Take you back quite soon.

'Your dog, it barked and woke you,
And that's what is to blame.
And you asked another thing.
Zomroh is my name.'

Joe could not believe his ears.
What had he just heard?
He was on board a spaceship?
It sounded so absurd.

He looked around and sure enough
The room he was inside
Looked to him like he had stepped
Into a fairground ride.

Round and white, this room was like
Nothing he had seen,
And at the front, on the wall,
An enormous screen.

Everywhere were banks of lights
Flashing all around,
Different colours, on and off,
Each making a sound.

And on the screen the lights and sounds
Formed a diagram,
A map to show where every woman,
And where every man,

And everybody in between
Was upon the globe,
And every baby newly born
Would make the lights all strobe.

And with a bleep computers spat out
Bits of information,
So that all the aliens could
Sit at their work station,

To go about examining
Every new statistic.
'Yes,' Joe thought, 'this spaceship
Is very futuristic.'

'Is this really real?' asked Joe,
And Zomroh turned around,
Waved its hand and suddenly
The screen, without a sound,

Changed into a window,
As big as big could be,
A window into outer space,
As far as Joe could see.

He shook his head. Was this a dream?
Was he still asleep?
He ran towards a tiny little window
For a peep.

And there so far below him,
The Earth so green and blue,
Confirmed this far-fetched story. Yes,
All of it was true!

And suddenly, like when he looked up
At the sky at night,
His fear turned to calm and he
Filled up with delight.

'WOW! THAT'S COOL,' Joe shouted,
And offered out his hand.
But Zomroh, as an alien,
Didn't understand.

'Hold your hand out just like me,
Then put your hand in mine.
On Earth it shows we're friends, you see,
We do it all the time.'

Zomroh looked uncertain,
But put its hand in Joe's
'Then we shake them up and down
So everybody knows

'We're friends, and sometimes friends do this!'
With that he gave a tug,
Pulled poor Zomroh close, and gave it
One almighty hug.

As you can imagine, Zomroh
Hadn't ever felt
A human hug, or ever met
A dog whose bottom smelt.

After what to Zomroh felt
Uncomfortably long,
The hugging stopped and Joe just smiled
Like nothing here was wrong.

Dusty had been watching Joe
Closely all this time,
Checking that he wasn't scared,
That everything was fine.

Once she saw Joe smile,
Knowing no harm was intended,
Dusty did her usual thing when
New friends she befriended,

And started wriggling on her back,
Her legs she held aloft,
Waiting for a tickle on her
Tummy, pink and soft.

Zomroh's eyes grew bigger. 'What is this?'
It said aloud,
And all the other aliens came
And gathered in a crowd.

'She's just being friendly,' Joe said.
'Let me show you how.'
He tickled Dusty on the tum and said,
'It's your turn now.'

Zomroh thought, 'I'll do it,'
Having never touched a dog.
So tickled her warm tummy
While the crew-mates stared, agog!

Up they got and Dusty sat,
Her tail wagged with joy,
Looking back and forth between
An alien and boy.

Joe thought Zomroh would have laughed
At such a funny game.
But no, the faces of the aliens
Were just the same.

Dusty made a happy, yelpy,
Growly funny sound,
Twisted this way, twisted that,
And wriggled all around.

Then up she jumped, excited,
Knocking Zomroh to the floor,
And licked and licked and licked its face
And then she licked some more.

Zomroh and the aliens,
They didn't really know
That these were doggy kisses,
And Dusty's way to show

That she was being friendly,
By acting like a fool,
Even if that meant she covered
Zomroh with her drool…

They didn't seem to be afraid,
They didn't seem amused,
They didn't smile or even frown,
They just seemed quite bemused.

In fact it seemed the aliens
Had quite an attitude,
So, 'That was fun,' said Joe to try to
Lighten up the mood.

'We have so much fun together,
Playing all the while.
Doesn't tickling Dusty make you
Even want to smile?'

But the aliens were quite confused
They'd never heard of 'fun'.
They didn't know the pleasure of
When a race is run,

Or the simple joy of playing games,
Or story-telling.
They just put facts inside their heads,
So that their brains kept swelling.

In fact, when you've got so much brain,
There is a consequence,
And that is why, you'll notice, that their heads
Are quite immense.

Over many years they'd let their
Feelings slip away,
They only wanted facts, which feelings
Sometimes could betray.

And over all those years, the things they
Thought of as distraction,
They left behind, for knowledge had
Become their great attraction.

As their feelings disappeared,
Other things did too.
They all became the same,
They didn't look like me or you.

There were no boys or girls, they didn't
Come in different colours,
Every single one of them
Looked just like the others.

With all feelings gone it put them
In the right position
To travel through the universe,
Observing was their mission.

And so these clever aliens
Could do most any thing,
Except for joke or hug or kiss,
They didn't dance or sing,

They didn't shout, they didn't cry,
And certainly they never
Laughed at farts, their brains were far too
Busy being clever.

They didn't feel emotions and, these days,
If truth be told,
    Where once had been a warm and beating heart
      Now just was cold.

      And that is why they didn't smile
      At Dusty or at Joe,
      For they'd forgotten how to smile
      A long, long time ago.

Chapter 5

The aliens could not deny that
There was a connection
Between this boy and dog, which gave
Zomroh some reflection.

The way they looked into each other's eyes,
As if they knew,
What the other thought about or
What they both would do,

Was something Zomroh had not seen,
Despite galactic travel.
And inside Zomroh, somewhere deep,
Things started to unravel.

Zomroh felt a stirring in the
Space inside its chest,
A fluttering, like baby birds
Singing in their nest.

Zomroh looked at Joe whose face was
Beaming with a grin.
So was Dusty's, making Zomroh stop
And stroke its chin.

And whilst it wondered what it was
That made their faces glow,
A teeny tiny feeling from within
Began to grow.

It came from Zomroh's tummy and
From its chest as well,
And though Zomroh didn't know it,
Its heart began to swell.

Zomroh hadn't seen a bond
Between a dog and boy,
And this tiny feeling was the start of something:
Joy!

'Zomroh, we must do our work,'
A voice said from the crew.
'Yes,' said Zomroh, knowing that
There was a lot to do.

'Joe, it's time to send you home
So we can make a start
With what we came to do here,
Before things fell apart.

'Sorry we can't study you,
This is our final visit.
We must say goodbye to Earth –
I think that I will miss it.

'We will make your mind forget
That you were ever here,
Because we have the power to make
Your memories disappear.

'You'll awake tomorrow back in bed,
You and your pup.
Then we'll finish why we came,
And blow your planet up!'

'Shush,' said all the aliens
And looked the other way.
'It's a secret Zomroh and
You're not supposed to say!'

45

'WHAT?' Joe shrieked as he and Dusty
Did a double take.
Surely what he thought he'd heard
Was simply a mistake.

'Did you just say you want to blow
The world up, is that right?'
Zomroh nodded. 'Yes, it should
Explode tomorrow night!'

'WHAT?' Joe shrieked again as Dusty
Hid behind her friend.
'Yes, that's right,' said Zomroh, 'so your
Time here now must end.'

'You can't blow the Earth up, and you
Haven't told me why
You came and took me from my bed
And up into the sky.

'And now you want to send me back!
Well first I'd like to know,
If you blow the Earth up, where will
Everybody go?

'What about my family, my friends
And everyone?
What will me and Dusty do
When everything has gone?'

The aliens fell silent and all
Looked down to the ground.
You could have heard a pin drop,
No one made a sound.

And once again from inside Zomroh
Something deep was shifting,
All the years of feeling nothing
Slowly started lifting.

Though it was strange, it seemed that having
Feelings wasn't bad,
Even if, like now, those feelings
Were a little sad.

Zomroh's brain was trying not to
Feel quite so harassed,
But for the first time ever…
Zomroh felt embarrassed.

47

'Well, you see,' said Zomroh, 'I was
Not supposed to mention
Blowing up your planet,
And now it's causing tension.

'I'm not supposed to say it,
I'm not supposed to tell.
When we blow up your planet,
We'll blow you all up as well!'

Joe was shocked! He could not quite
Believe what he had heard.
He had to stop and think it through,
It all seemed so absurd.

Even Dusty sensed that something
Really wasn't right.
She popped her tail between her legs
And hid just out of sight.

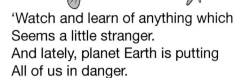

'Why?' said Joe. 'What have people
Ever done to you?
And what about the animals,
The trees and fishes too?'

An alien stepped forward saying,
In a tiny voice,
'Show him, Zomroh, show him that
We do not have a choice.'

Zomroh turned and images
Appeared on the screen.
'These will help to show you whilst
I tell you what we mean.

'We travel through the cosmos,
So that we can preserve
Peace throughout the universe.
And so we must observe,

'Watch and learn of anything which
Seems a little stranger.
And lately, planet Earth is putting
All of us in danger.

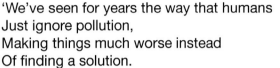

'We've seen for years the way that humans
Just ignore pollution,
Making things much worse instead
Of finding a solution.

'It seemed to us the human race was
Bent on self-destruction.
"Leave them to get on with it,"
That was our instruction.

'But something different happened,
We noticed something change –
Very odd behaviour that we
Found was very strange.

'Humans all around the world
Becoming more aggressive,
And so we made this plan, which we think
Is quite impressive.

'Because we know this change is simply
One we can't ignore.
We know you're training soldiers
And intend to start a war!

'Millions learning how to fight
With your technology,
A war with all the aliens
Throughout the galaxy.

'We've seen you at your consoles,
Watching as you learn
How to fight and shoot us, and it
Causes much concern.

'We've watched you learning how to blow
Our spaceships into bits,
So you can imagine how
Uneasily that sits.

'When we beam a person up we
Look inside their mind,
And what humans want to do to us,
It isn't very kind.

'And so we have to stop you
Before it is too late,
And blowing up your planet –
That should do the job just great!'

And all the aliens agreed,
Like members of a jury.
But on the screen, the images told
Quite a different story.

As Joe watched what was on the screen
It all became quite clear,
The aliens had got it wrong
And had nothing to fear.

For what they had been witnessing,
What they had mistaken,
As training for a war from minds
Of people they had taken,

Through peeking in the windows of
All those girls and boys,
Wasn't training for a war,
But children playing with their toys!

People on their phones, their tablets,
Their computer screens,
Playing games by blowing aliens
To smithereens.

Guns and big explosions,
Consoles gripped so tight,
Fighting off the alien invaders
Every night.

People like Joe's friends all gamed,
And his sister too.
People all around the world,
People just like you.

And if you think about it,
It's not a big surprise,
The aliens believed what they
Could see with their own eyes.

Remember that the aliens were
Very scientific,
They just looked at evidence and
Things that were specific.

They didn't have a way to see that
People found it fun,
To kill computer aliens
With a computer gun.

For them there were no games, no playing,
Laughter, joy or mirth,
And so they had concluded they must
Blow up planet Earth.

Chapter 6

'Wait.' said Joe. 'you've got it wrong -
You've made a big mistake.
None of that is real.
It's just a game. It's fake.

'That's just people having fun,
They aren't in an army.
Blowing up the planet Earth for that
Would just be barmy!'

The aliens looked puzzled,
And Zomroh said, bemused,
'Games? We do not understand
And now we're quite confused.

'What is all this "having fun"?
Can you please explain?
We've never tried to look for "fun"
Inside a human brain.'

This presented Joe with quite
A problem actually,
Showing that there's such a thing as
Fun and joy and glee.

How do you show someone this
Or prove these things are real?
Thing's that you don't think about,
But something that you feel?

If Joe was going to save the world
From going in a blast,
He'd have to do it quickly,
Time was ticking fast!

Joe looked down at Dusty
And that gave him a clue,
Maybe playing games with her
Was just the thing to do?

When they played, it filled their hearts
Like they were going to burst,
And Dusty always knew when Joe
Was feeling at his worst.

She could turn his feelings right around
From low to high.
So Joe decided this was something
Worth giving a try.

'Right,' said Joe, 'we'll show you what it
Means to have a laugh.'
'Excellent,' said Zomroh,
'Will we need to draw a graph?'

'No,' said Joe, 'now gather round for
This could take a while.
The first thing that we have to do
Is teach you how to smile.'

So all the little aliens
Gathered round to see,
For what Joe said had woken up
Their curiosity.

'First you stretch your lips so that
Your teeth are all on show,
Raise your eyebrows really high
And then you're good to go!'

Joe was pretty nervous, well,
How else could he feel?
He looked more like a puppet,
As his smile wasn't real.

Still the aliens all tried
To copy what they saw,
Moving lips and eyes in ways
They never had before.

But they had a problem, as they
Just did not know how
To make your eyebrows smile when
Your eyes don't have a brow.

So they just showed their little teeth,
Opened wide their eyes,
It didn't look like smiling,
It looked more like surprise.

So Joe looked down at Dusty.
'Show them how,' he said.
But when Dusty showed her teeth,
They turned around and fled!

They huddled in their corner,
But Zomroh didn't run.
In fact, this made the alien
Start to feel fun.

Frightening the aliens,
That made Zomroh grin,
And it wasn't just pretend,
This smile was genuine.

'That's it there, that's a smile,'
Joe shouted happily.
An alien's first smile,
For everyone to see.

Never having witnessed this,
The aliens came looking,
As inside Zomroh, something really
Wonderful was cooking.

'Oooohhh,' said all the aliens,
Seeing Zomroh's face.
Joe knew now that he and Dusty
Must pick up the pace.

'Even though these games of war
Are horrible, it's true,
They aren't real so, Dusty, this is
What we have to do.

'We have to make them see it's all
Just a silly game.
If we don't, they'll blow us up
And that would be a shame.

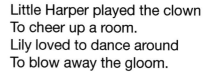

'We have to make them laugh,' said Joe,
Trying hard to think
Of things he found hilarious.
And then, within a blink,

It came to him that all his sisters
Made him laugh out loud,
Each one in a different way
Could lift a heavy cloud.

Little Harper played the clown
To cheer up a room.
Lily loved to dance around
To blow away the gloom.

And Skye made sure that everyone
Felt part of a team.
Feeling you're included, that can
Really make you beam.

'Dusty, roll around, get on your back
To make them giggle.'
Dusty turned and rolled around and did
Her doggy wriggle.

Acting like a pair of clowns they
Tried to raise a grin.
But very soon, it was clear
They were not going to win.

Even when Joe tickled Dusty,
All over her tummy,
Zomroh was the only one who
Found it vaguely funny.

Why was that? Why was Zomroh
Different from the rest?
Touching Joe and Dusty melted
What was in its chest.

Slowly Zomroh's frozen heart
Was starting to thaw out,
Giving it a taste of what these
"Feelings" were about.

But what to do, now that clowning
Didn't really work?
It didn't make them smile,
It didn't raise a smirk.

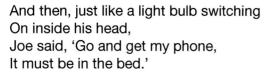

And then, just like a light bulb switching
On inside his head,
Joe said, 'Go and get my phone,
It must be in the bed.'

Pricking up her ears, as if
Searching for a bone,
Dusty ran like lightning
To fetch Joe's mobile phone.

Her superpowered sniffing very
Soon picked up the trail,
Leading back towards the room where,
With her wagging tail,

Dusty leapt upon the bed
And soon the phone was found,
Underneath Joe's pillow, where this
Gentle little hound

Used her mouth to pick it up
And take it back to Joe.
What he was going to do with it,
That, she did not know.

And as Joe wiped the slobber from her mouth
From off his phone,
Realising acting like a clown
Could not alone

Teach the aliens what having
Fun is meant to be,
Maybe something else could.
Maybe music was the key!

Chapter 7

On his phone Joe found his favourite playlist
Titled DANCE!
Took a breath and held it high -
This could be Earth's last chance.

He and Dusty stomped into
The middle of the floor,
The aliens without a clue
Of what they had in store.

Then he hit the button and his
Song began to play,
Getting Joe's feet tapping, in his arms
A gentle sway.

Then dancing all around to
The rhythm of the beat,
Twirling, jumping up and down,
Stomping with his feet.

Spinning to the music, dancing
Like his little sister -
Dipping, waving, singing, laughing,
Swirling like a twister!

Dusty turning circles, swaying,
Barking with the song.
But something wasn't working,
Something still was wrong.

When the song had finished Joe could
See this task was tough.
But there was still one thing to try,
'It's not loud enough!

'Surely you can make the wifi
And my phone connect.
We're trying really hard here!
We've a planet to protect!'

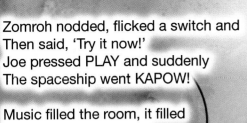

Zomroh nodded, flicked a switch and
Then said, 'Try it now!'
Joe pressed PLAY and suddenly
The spaceship went KAPOW!

Music filled the room, it filled
The corridors and halls.
You could feel vibrations,
Music bouncing off the walls.

All at once the aliens could
Feel the music too.
Joe could see that some were even
Learning what to do.

Over there, an alien had
Gently started nodding,
One was lifting up its feet,
In a kind of plodding.

One was strumming to the beat
With fingers long and thin,
And when Joe looked at Zomroh,
He saw a massive grin!

Suddenly from nowhere
Zomroh leapt into the air,
Ran and cuddled Joe and started
Dancing without care.

'Though I'd heard of feelings
I thought they were a rumour,
But it turns out that they're real and
I've got a sense of humour!'

Then, as with many songs, there was
A quiet interlude,
A bit right in the middle
That helps to build the mood,

Like when you know a train is coming,
Speeding through a station,
Building up excitement to
Create anticipation.

Zomroh, filled with new sensations,
Said, grabbing Joe's hand,
'So this is what fun feels like.
Now I understand!

Then the music hit and BANG!
Everybody jumped,
Everybody danced and moved
As the music thumped.

It was like the aliens had drunk
A magic potion,
Something changing in them,
Something called emotion.

'Look at that,' Joe shouted, pointing,
'Wow, that's really weird!'
As there, on all the spaceship's screens,
His photographs appeared!

'Hey, let's have a selfie, Zomroh,'
Joe said to his chum.
'Smile at the camera
And show us all your thumb.'

Zomroh didn't have a thumb,
So they just hugged instead.
Then the selfie showed up on
The big screen overhead.

All the aliens, amazed,
Wanted selfies too,
There were quite a lot of them,
They had to form a queue.

And as the music carried on,
All the dancing too,
Photographs of Joe and Dusty
And the friends they knew,

Having fun together, laughing,
Playing with each other,
Photos of them cuddling with Joe's sisters,
Dad and mother,

These became like signals going
Into outer space,
Sending aliens a different view
Of the human race.

So for a while this spaceship,
Sent to blow us up,
Transformed into a disco,
As this boy and his pup

Somehow changed these aliens,
A change that was profound.
Amazing what a child can do,
And their trusty hound.

But so much fun was being had,
They didn't hear at all,
The sound of heavy footsteps
Marching down the hall.

Pausing in the doorway stood a
Figure looking cross,
A bigger creature altogether.
Hello, Zomroh's boss…

Chapter 8

Before, I said these aliens were
All the same, it's true.
But this bigger alien's
What happened when they grew.

This alien was older, wiser,
Mainly, it was large.
And the most important thing?
It was the one in charge.

Noticing this crew had not been
Sending their report,
The boss beamed down in a machine,
Called a teleport,

To find out what was happening,
What could be the fault,
What was bringing all their plans
Grinding to a halt?

And as it stood there watching
From just inside the door,
The alien could not believe
Exactly what it saw.

Everyone was laughing, dancing,
Music playing loud.
And so that great big alien
Moved towards the crowd.

One by one they saw it as it
Slowly came inside.
They bowed their heads and looked away,
Others tried to hide,

Until they'd all stopped dancing
And stood still as still could be.
But Dusty, Joe and Zomroh
Were the final three.

With music playing loudly,
They danced without a care,
They didn't have a clue, they were
Completely unaware.

The alien looked down and said,
In a gentle tone,
'Excuse me, could you stop that noise
Coming from your phone?'

'That's not noise, it's music,'
Zomroh said, not noticing
That now the other aliens
Were all quivering.

Dusty noticed next and started
Tugging at Joe's sleeve,
Pulling him away as if it
Was now time to leave.

'Dusty, what's the matter?
Isn't this the best of fun?
I think we'll be OK now that
We're friends with everyone!'

But Dusty shook her head and Joe
Turned around to see
The biggest, tallest alien
Ever there could be.

69

All that Joe could do was gulp
And switch the music off,
Signalling to Zomroh with a
Nervous little cough.

'That was so much fun!' said Zomroh.
'I enjoyed the feeling.'
But Joe just stared and nodded,
Up towards the ceiling.

Zomroh jumped with great surprise,
A mile into the air.
Looking at the alien, who said,
'Well, I despair!

'Explain to me exactly why
Your mission is delayed.
Everybody back at home is
Really quite dismayed.'

The alien let out a sigh
And it shook its head.
'And someone tell me why this boy and
Dog are here,' it said.

It felt like when in classrooms,
Kids make a mighty din,
But everyone goes silent when
The teacher marches in.

And that's because the aliens
All felt slightly queer,
Now they understood emotions,
They were feeling fear.

With a slightly wobbly voice,
Poor Zomroh meekly spoke.
'We beamed up one more human, Joe,
Then his dog awoke.

'She had us cornered until Joe
Came and rescued us.
Before we knew it, we forgot the
Mission, that's because

'Joe and Dusty showed us what it's like
To feel good.
We've never felt like this, we didn't
Even know we could!

'And so we put the plans to blow the
Earth up to an end.
'Cos Joe and Dusty showed us
What it's like to have a friend.'

But the big boss alien was
Not at all amused.
'I don't understand it, I'm
Feeling quite confused.

'What is all this movement?
These smiles I can see?'
Joe stepped gently forward, saying,
'That's because of me.

'I was only trying to show my friends
What it's like to feel.
Show them that computer games –
They aren't even real.

'Sorry we messed up your plan,
But I don't think it's right
To blow my home and all my friends
To bits tomorrow night.'

The alien's eyes softened as
It looked down at Joe.
'I'm so sorry for this mess,
But now you have to go.

'We have to blow the planet up,
I know that seems unkind,
But first I'll wipe your memory,
And take this from your mind.

'In the morning you'll wake up,
Both you and your hound,
You won't remember anything.
Now, how does all that sound?'

'Not so nice at all,' said Joe
'Not a little bit.'
The alien looked up and said,
'Well, let's get on with it.

'Joe, we'll take you to your bed
And it won't hurt at all.
I'll put my fingers on your head,
And then asleep you'll fall.

'When you wake, you'll remember
Nothing about me,
Nothing about Zomroh or the others,
Wait and see.'

The aliens all looked around,
Feeling rather sad,
They hadn't known that feelings,
Could be both good and bad.

'But what about my friends?' said Joe,
'And my family?
Everyone I know is going to
Disappear with me!'

'Joe, we're in a hurry here so
Let me make this brief.
Say goodbye to everyone,
I've spoken, I'm the Chief!'

And so it seemed that Joe and Dusty's
Story had unfurled.
But not as they hoped for –
They hadn't saved the world!

Chapter 9

Everybody gathered in a circle
Round the bed.
But Joe first turned to Zomroh
And this is what he said.

'Zomroh, thanks for showing me
The things I did not know.
We could have been best friends
If I didn't have to go.

'Before I do, you have to know,
I'm very glad we met.
And now I need to ask you something.
Would you like a pet?'

'What?' thought Dusty, ears pricked up.
'Joe surely can't mean me.'
But with no other pets around
Who else could it be?

Dusty walked to Joe with an
Expression of surprise.
Joe got down upon his knees
And looked into her eyes.

'You have always been there for me
When I'm feeling low,
Making me feel better because,
Somehow, you just know!

'Even when I'm happy you can
Make me brighter still.
I have always loved you, Dusty,
And I always will.

'Dusty, you're my closest friend
In all the world, it's true,
But I can't take you home with me.
So this is what we'll do.

'You'll stay here with Zomroh,
They'll all look after you.
If you come back to Earth with me,
You'll get blown up too.

'I can't let that happen so
I need you to be brave.
Dusty, it's so hard but you're the
One friend I can save.'

Dusty moved in close to Joe,
In her eye, a tear.
Joe held her in the biggest hug
And whispered in her ear.

'I always wished that you could talk,
And that we'd never part.
But now we have to say goodbye,
Although it breaks my heart.'

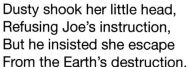

Dusty shook her little head,
Refusing Joe's instruction,
But he insisted she escape
From the Earth's destruction.

She nuzzled at Joe's neck and sniffed
His scent so she'd remember
That love can set your heart on fire
From just a tiny ember.

She raised her head up high and howled,
Such a sad, sad sound.
Then something quite remarkable
Happened all around.

Every single alien,
(Not the boss of course),
Felt heartbreak for the first time ever,
With a mighty force.

After many centuries of
Eyes forever dry,
Every single one of them
Now began to cry.

Their little hearts erupted
With feelings so intense.
They were really overwhelmed.
These feelings were immense.

They had travelled everywhere,
Seen most everything,
But what's the point when deep inside
Your feelings cannot sing?

Now their hearts had melted and they
Knew what feelings were.
Joe and Dusty showed them what
It feels like to care.

And so the alien in charge
Looked across the crew,
Sobbing, holding others up.
What a big to-do!

And yet, there was a tiny spark
Lighting up within,
And from its chest it turned into
A tremble of its chin.

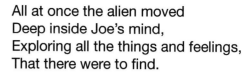

It had not experienced,
In a thousand years,
Anything so powerful
As Joe and Dusty's tears!

And, like all good scientists,
When something that is new
Presents itself, investigating
Is the thing to do.

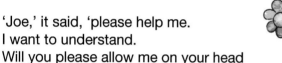

'Joe,' it said, 'please help me.
I want to understand.
Will you please allow me on your head
To place my hand?'

Joe looked up, he wasn't sure.
Could this be a trick?
To wipe away his memory and
Send him back home, quick?

But if there was a single chance
Joe must take it now,
So he grabbed the great big hand
And placed it on his brow.

All at once the alien moved
Deep inside Joe's mind,
Exploring all the things and feelings,
That there were to find.

And what it found was quite unique for,
Never once before,
Had it come across a mind
Which felt so very pure.

Joe was free of anger, hatred,
Violence or rage.
These were things the alien
Had seen in kids his age.

Joe was full of kindness, fun,
His mind was filled with joy.
The alien could see Joe was
A very special boy.

It saw the fun of make-believe which
Made it see the truth –
The games they thought were real were not.
Joe's mind was the proof.

But something else was there within,
Bigger, honest, true.
The alien, not knowing why,
Reached for Dusty too.

Straight away a lightning bolt
Shot between the pair,
Meeting in the middle of
The alien, right where,

Once a heart devoid of feeling,
Suddenly was full,
Of this love between a boy
And his English Bull.

Zomroh held Joe's other hand
And everyone joined in,
Forming one big circle so the
Magic could begin.

All the love that flowed between this
Boy and his best friend
Felt bigger than the universe
Stretched from end to end.

And so at last they understood,
Now they were complete,
Love's the strongest thing there is,
There's nothing it can't beat.

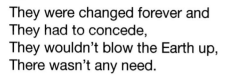

They were changed forever and
They had to concede,
They wouldn't blow the Earth up,
There wasn't any need.

And with that announcement,
They all cheered hip hooray,
For Earth and all its people would not
Get blown up today!

So Joe and Dusty would go home,
Sworn to secrecy.
Selfies all deleted
So nobody would see.

Joe said goodbye to everyone
But Zomroh was the last.
They smiled and hugged, and Joe felt that,
Somewhere in the vast

Reaches of the galaxy,
That a time would come,
When Zomroh could be introduced
To his dad and mum.

As if, in many years from now,
They might meet once more,
A friend beyond the universe
Knocking on Joe's door.

'Thank you both,' said Zomroh.
'You showed me what to do.
Now I can dance and laugh and feel
All because of you.

'You both have a special place
In my memory,
I will not forget you.
Please remember me.'

And for these friends from different worlds,
It was time to part.
But now these clever aliens
Had feelings in their hearts.

Hometime now for boy and dog,
And so, with goodbyes said,
Joe and Dusty waited, hugging,
Lying in their bed.

Just before Joe closed his eyes
To start the journey home,
The big chief alien sat down
And said, 'Now we're alone,

'I thank you for the lessons that we
Have all learned from you.
We'd forgotten how to feel
But now we will be true,

'And listen to our hearts as well as
All that we can learn.
What a gift! So now I offer
Something in return.

'Joe, when I was in your mind
I saw two wishes there,
But I can grant just one of them,
So please now take great care.

'You must make a choice, for only
One wish can come true.
As you sleep I'll look once more
And know just what to do.

'So close your eyes and go to sleep.
Tomorrow you'll awake,
Knowing that you saved the world
From such a big mistake.'

Amazingly the alien
Had found out something true,
Joe's old wish remained but now
He had a new one too.

Joe thought hard about his wishes.
One, he'd have to keep.
The alien kissed Joe and Dusty,
And then they fell asleep.

Chapter 10

So the morning came and woke up Joe
With gentle light.
He yawned, he stretched and rubbed his eyes.
Goodness, what a night!

Was it all imagination?
Was it all a dream?
Just then, from the room next door,
He heard his sister scream.

What could be the matter with her?
What sent Skye berserk?
Then he heard her shouting,
'My computer game won't work!'

Joe's mum came into the room
And tousled with his hair.
Never had he been so happy
Just to have her there.

Thinking of what might have been
Because of such a muddle.
Joe filled with emotion
And gave his mum a cuddle.

'Mum, I love you, and I love
My sisters and my dad.'
Mum looked down and smiled and said,
'Well, I'm very glad,

'Because we love you too, you know.
You're our special boy.'
They hugged and hugged for ages,
Filling them with joy.

'What's the matter with Skye's game?'
Joe asked curiously.
'Something strange – they're talking all
About it on TV!'

And so it was, throughout the world,
Each computer game
Had changed itself and, from now on,
Would never be the same.

Where there once were guns and lasers,
Bullets, noise and dread,
There were phones in people's hands and
Music played instead.

Where there once were armies fighting
Aliens at war,
Everyone was dancing like they'd
Never danced before.

Scoring points by adding up the
Selfies you could click,
With a friendly alien
Who had a selfie stick.

Nobody threw hand grenades,
They all threw pretty flowers.
Now people who played games were nice
For hours and hours and hours.

And though it took a little time,
People liked it more
When aliens and people danced,
Instead of making war.

Joe sat back and smiled. He was
The only one who knew,
How those clever aliens
Made his new wish come true.

Still, his other wish was one he'd
Had to sacrifice.
It seemed that doing something good
Came at quite a price.

That's when Dusty woke up too
From by Joe's smelly feet.
She made her way up to him, poked her
Head out from the sheet.

She looked into Joe's eyes
And they curled up in the bed.
Their adventure now was over.
'I love you girl,' he said.

'I love you too,' she said right back,
Much to Joe's delight.
'Guess what? You're not the only one
Whose wish came true last night!'

Joe could not believe his ears.
Could this all be real?
Aliens made wishes happen
Now that they could feel.

The two of them, they hugged and kissed,
And held each other tight.
Who'd have thought that they could change the world
In just one night!

And so the love that Joe and Dusty had
Just grew and grew.
They talked a lot but secretly –
No one ever knew.

They'd have many more adventures,
Side by side, a team.
With their loving family,
Life was like a dream.

And so remember, in the end,
It's not just being smart
That saves us all, it is revealing
What is in your heart.

It isn't who is strongest or
Who has a bigger gun,
Being cruel to others
Because you think it's fun.

It isn't being violent,
Angry, mean or rude,
It is about a warmer,
Very different attitude.

For Joe may not have been a boy
Who did so well at tests,
But he had many other skills
To stand out from the rest,

Like his loving, caring nature.
That was more his role.
Joe had something really special –
Kindness in his soul.

Boys and girls like Joe are always
More than they are labelled.
Everyone, in some way,
Can be differently abled.

For though it would be great to have
Abilities astounding,
Like flying through the air,
Gravity confounding,

Being strong, invisible or fast
Just like a jet,
There's something that we do all have
That we should not forget.

It's right there in all of us,
Above all else it towers,
Stronger and more wonderful
Than any superpowers.

Joe and Dusty always had it,
Bonding them like glue,
And guess what? You are just like them,
Because you have it too.

And it was all that mattered when
A threat came from above,
For Joe and Dusty saved the world,
They saved the world with love.

THE END

Thank you!

Thanks to everyone who contributed to the GoFundMe campaign to publish hardback versions of Joe and Dusty Save the World, so that up to 10% could be given away for free. Our top supporters are:

Hormoz Ahmadzadeh Andy, Lee, Lloyd and Eleanor Jane Cordell

Edwin de la Cruz Rüdiger Dehn

Julie Hesmondhalgh Soraya Letterie Adrian Mills

Richard Nutter Result CIC

Ravi and Rick Caitriona Vulliamy John Williams

Huge thanks to my collaborators on this book, **Margit van der Zwan**, for bringing the story to life with her beautiful illustrations, and **Anne Louise Kershaw** for her gorgeous design. Thanks also to Lesley Levine, Harriet Williams, Jackie Driver and Teresa Wilson for help, advice and support, to Francesca, Scott and my family for their invaluable feedback, and to my husband Hormoz, for letting me test out the rhymes on him and for always believing in me.